What the Grizzly Knows

What the Grizzly Knows

David Elliott

illustrated by Max Grafe

CANDLEWICK PRESS
CAMBRIDGE, MASSACHUSETTS

The lights are out.
You're snug in bed
with Teddy
nestled at your head.

The moon's
a saucer full of cream,
you think
as you begin to dream,

when there, before
your half-closed eyes,
Teddy starts
to change his size.

Teddy growls
as Teddy grows;
Teddy pops
his button nose . . .

and in its place?
A grizzly snout.
Bear within
and bear without.

Ivory claws
click on the floor

as the bear moves
toward the door,

where he stands
and waits for you.
For you've become
a grizzly, too.

Now two bears –
one big, one small –
amble down
the upstairs hall,

which fades into
a forest track.
The stars are bright,
the shadows black.

Sure-footed
on high grizzly ledges,

you feast upon
the mountain sedges,

and there
in icy grizzly streams,
you fish the waters
of your dreams.

Throughout the night
you roam and prowl.
You see the fox;
you hear the owl,

watchful
from her feathered nest.
A grizzly's heart
beats in your chest.

Throughout the night,
you prowl and roam;

the forest has
become your home.

When morning's sun
dispels the gloom,
he leads you back,
back to your room,

to leave the dreamy world,
so wild–

bear no longer,
now a child.

No one will guess;
no one will find
the bear prints
that you've left behind.

And none but Teddy
will suppose
that you know
what the grizzly knows.

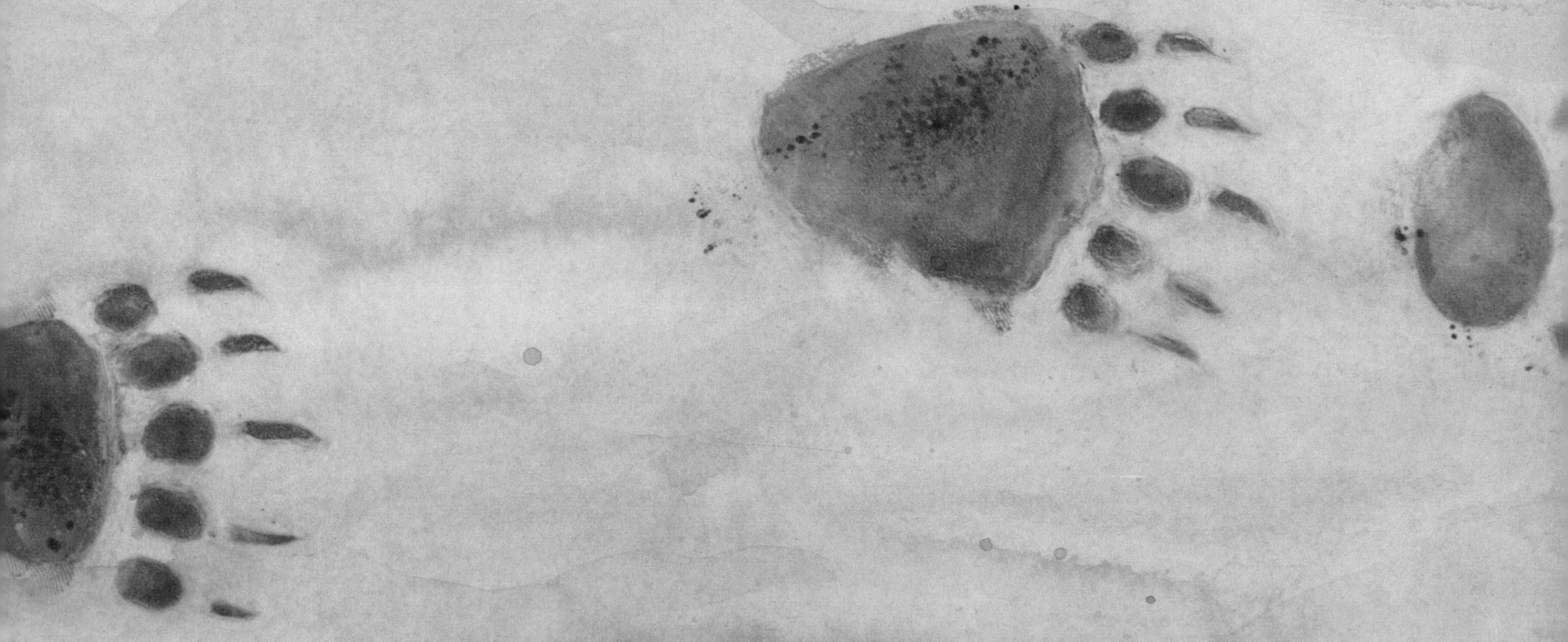

To Liz Bicknell, a dream of an editor
D. E.

For my sparrow, the fluttering Tifenn,
and for ones who will always live in my heart, Mom and Dad
M. G.

First edition 2008

Library of Congress Cataloging-in-Publication Data is available.

Library of Congress Catalog Card Number 2007052158

ISBN 978-0-7636-2778-2

2 4 6 8 10 9 7 5 3 1

Printed in China

This book was typeset in Mithras.
The illustrations were done in monotype, drypoint etching, and watercolor.

Candlewick Press
2067 Massachusetts Avenue
Cambridge, Massachusetts 02140

visit us at www.candlewick.com